YOUR PET STEGOSAURUS

By Kirsty Holmes

WINDMILL BOOKS

Published in 2019 by Windmill Books,
an Imprint of Rosen Publishing
29 East 21st Street, New York, NY 10010

Editor: Madeline Tyler
Book Design: Danielle Jones

Cataloging-in-Publication Data

Names: Holmes, Kirsty.
Title: Your pet stegosaurus / Kirsty Holmes.
Description: New York : Windmill Books, 2019. | Series: How to care for your pet dinosaur | Includes glossary and index.
Identifiers: ISBN 9781538391105 (pbk.) | ISBN 9781508197614 (library bound) | ISBN 9781538391112 (6 pack)
Subjects: LCSH: Stegosaurus--Juvenile literature. | Dinosaurs--Juvenile literature.
Classification: LCC QE862.O65 H645 2019 | DDC 567.915'3--dc23

Manufactured in the United States of America

CPSIA Compliance Information: Batch BW19WM: For Further Information contact Rosen Publishing, New York, New York at 1-800-237-9932

IMAGE CREDITS

Cover – solar22, Bibela, ONYXprj, stuckmotion, isaree, Kurt Natalia. 1 & throughout – Sentavio, stuckmotion, solar22. 4 – VasiliyArt. 5 – Sentavio. 8 – Banana Walking, GoodStudio. 9 – Mironova Iuliia. 12 – Shany Muchnik, paprika, SofiaV. 13 – Elvetica. 14–15 – elenabsl. 17 – AlexBocharov. 20 – VectorShow. 21 – nuvrenia. Images are courtesy of Shutterstock.com. With thanks to Getty Images, Thinkstock Photo and iStockphoto.

CONTENTS

THE OFFICIAL F.O.S.S.I.L GUIDE

Words that look like this can be found in the glossary on page 24.

F.O.S.S.I.L

So, you're the proud owner of a dinosaur egg. Congratulations!

Owning a pet dinosaur is a lot of hard work, but it's worth the trouble. Dinosaurs make excellent pets.

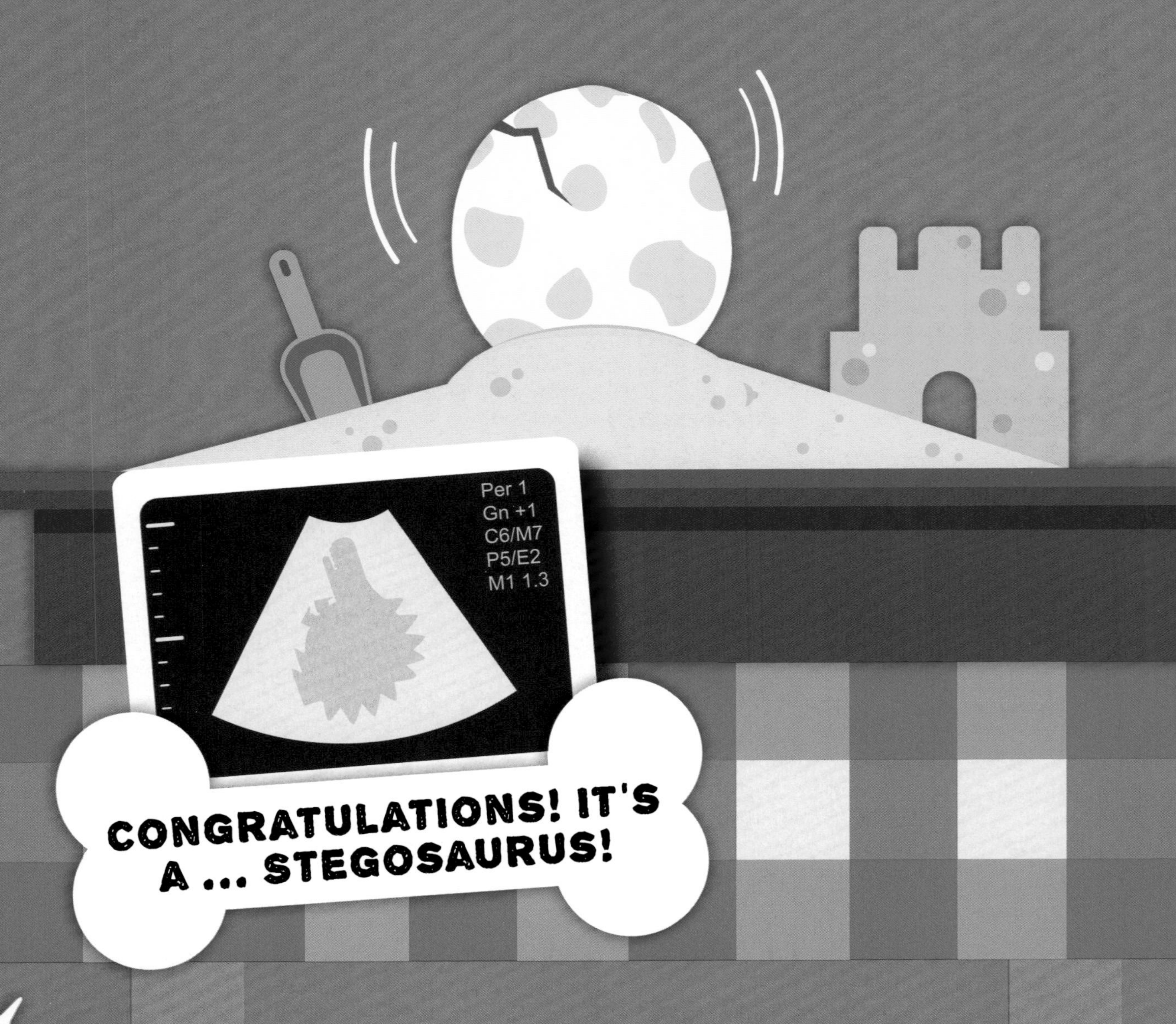

If you are a first-time dinosaur owner, you probably have lots of questions. Never fear! This handy F.O.S.S.I.L guide will tell you all you need to know.

F.O.S.S.I.L FACT

F.O.S.S.I.L stands for:

Federal
Office of
Super
Sized
Interesting
Lovable reptiles

EGGS

Stegosaurus eggs are spherical. They are about 4 inches (11 cm) wide.

4 INCHES

Stegosaurus eggs should be kept in a shallow nest, dug into some sand.

YOUR EGG WILL DO WELL IF KEPT WARM, SO BUILD YOUR NEST IN A SUNNY PLACE.

BABIES

When it hatches, your Stegosaurus will be around the size of a kitten. Keep your pet in a closed, quiet room at first. They will be quite shy.

YOUR PET WILL NEED SOME TOYS AND A LITTER BOX.

Feed your Stegosaurus mosses and ferns. A Stegosaurus doesn't have a strong bite, so go ahead and feed your pet from your hands.

GROWTH

Your Stegosaurus will grow slowly and steadily. Babies are around the size of cats. Teenagers are around 18.5 feet (5.6 m) long, and 8 feet (2.5 m) tall.

BABY

Adults can grow as long as 30 feet (9 m) and weigh up to 7.7 tons (7 t). This is very heavy, so it might not be a good idea to let your Stegosaurus live upstairs.

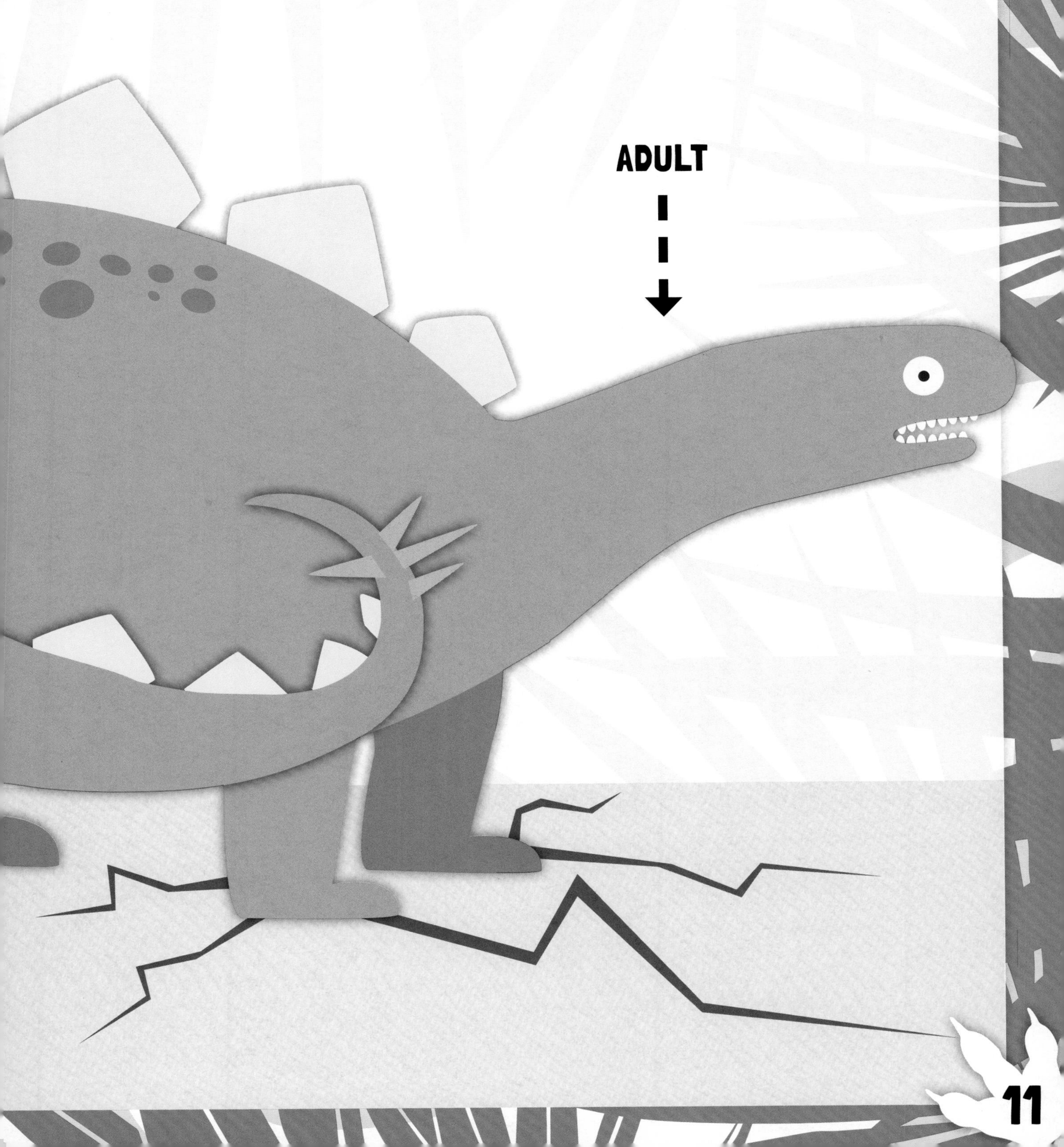

FOOD

Stegosaurs are herbivores, which means they only eat plants. They have small teeth and a weak bite.

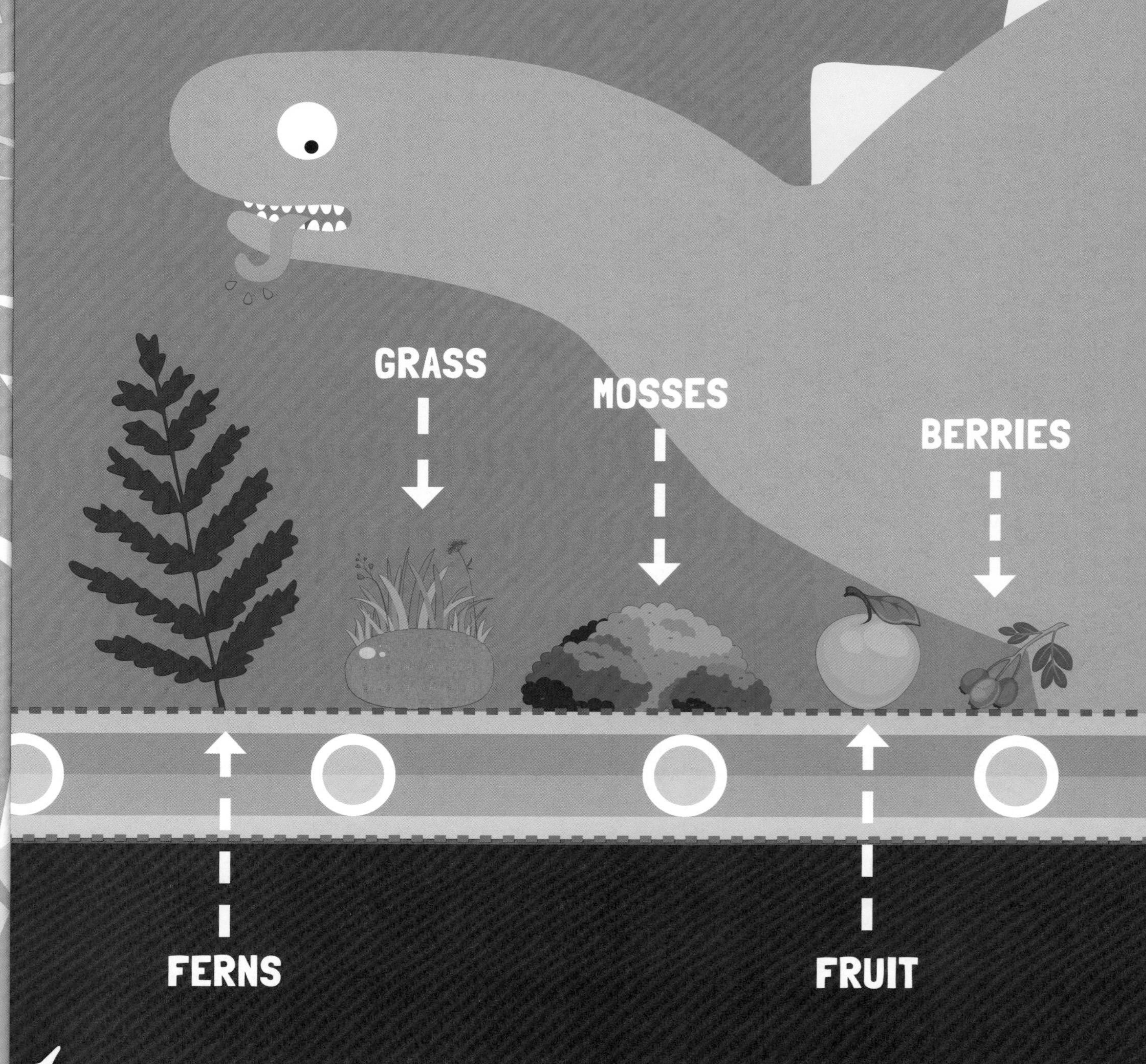

Because its teeth are so small, your Stegosaurus might eat small stones. These are called gastroliths and roll around in the stomach to help the Stegosaurus digest its food.

EXERCISE

Your Stegosaurus won't need much exercise. They walk very slowly and spend most of the day eating. Try a gentle walk around the park if your pet is in the mood.

Stegosaurus has long spikes on the end of its tail. It is safest to stay at the front of your pet when going for walks to avoid being hit.

FOSSIL FACT
Your Stegosaurus will walk slowly but is very heavy. Don't let them walk on your toes!

NAMING

Naming your Stegosaurus is very important when bonding with your pet. You could choose to use the first letter, S, when choosing a name.

SOPHIE

FOSSIL FACT

What will you name your Stegosaurus?

You could use words that describe your Stegosaurus to name it instead. Stegosaurus has huge armored plates and a spiky tail.

WASHING

It is important that you keep your pet clean, especially between its plates. You will need:

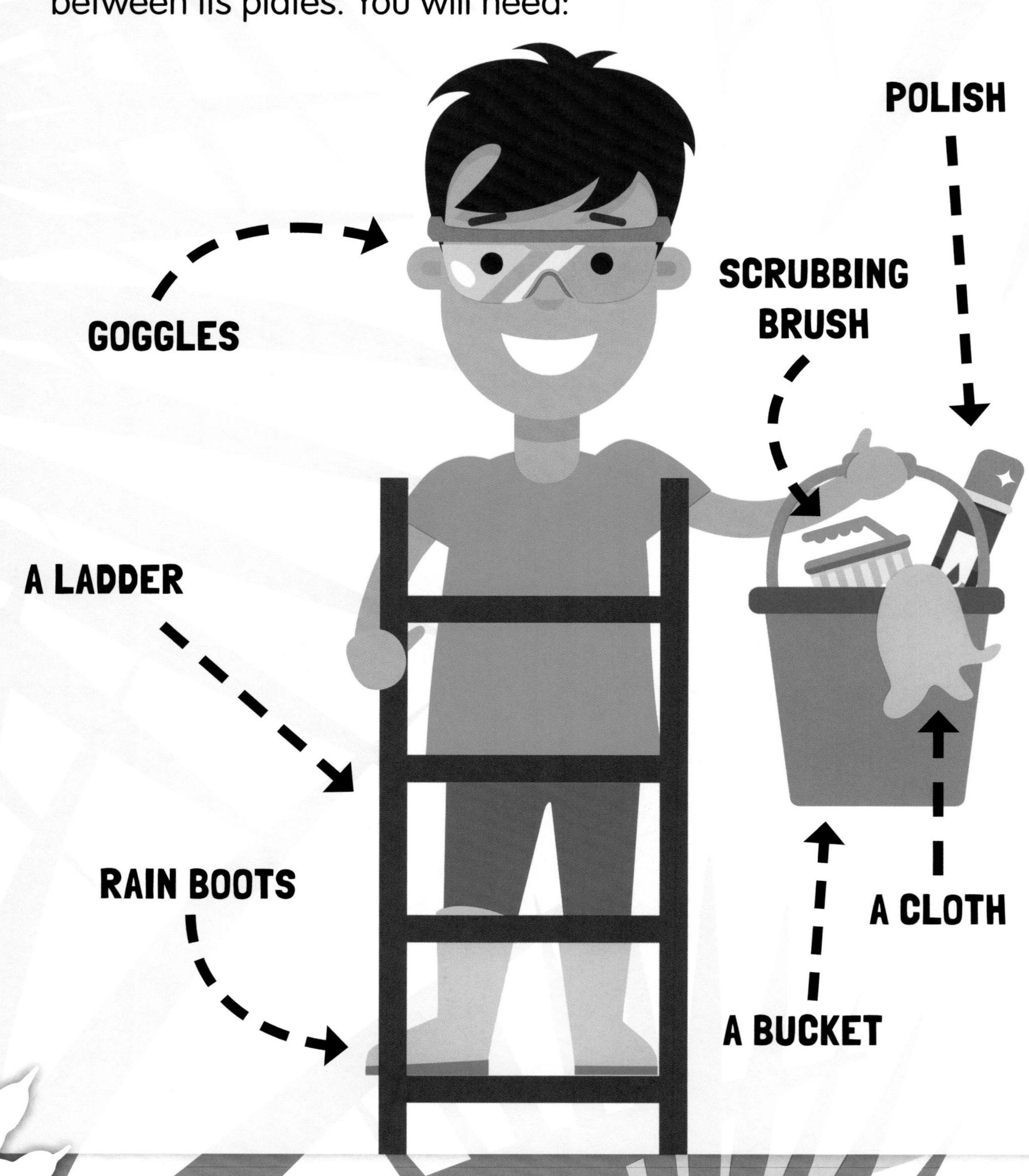

Make sure to carefully polish the plates to a nice shine. This will bring out the colors.

PROBLEMS

Stegosaurus has a small brain – only about as big as a walnut. This means they aren't very bright and can easily get into trouble.

WE RECOMMEND KEEPING A CLOSE EYE ON YOUR PET.

One problem with herbivores is that they make a lot of… well… gas. That's another good reason to stay at the front end of your pet at all times.

TRICKS

Since your Stegosaurus won't be the smartest pet, it won't learn tricks easily. However, you can try climbing onto its back using its armored plates.

THERE ARE HOURS OF FUN TO BE HAD WITH YOUR FRIENDLY NEW PET!

Stegosaurus will love to learn a few simple commands. If you can be patient, it is very rewarding.

GLOSSARY

ARMORED covered in a protective layer, called armor

BONDING forming a close relationship

DIGEST break down food into things that can be used by the body

HATCHES when a baby animal comes out of its egg

MOSSES small, flowerless plants that grow in clumps

NEST any place used by an animal to lay eggs or rear young

SHALLOW not deep

SPHERICAL shaped like a ball

INDEX